The Clever Boy and the Terrible, Dangerous Animal

By Idries Shah

Once upon a time there was a very clever boy who lived in a village.

Nearby was another village that he had never visited.

When he was old enough to be allowed to go about on his own, he thought he would like to see the other village.

So one day, he asked his mother if he could go, and she said, "Yes, as long as you look both ways before you cross the road. You must be very careful!"

The boy agreed and set off at once. When he got to the side of the road, he looked both ways. And because there was nothing coming, he knew he could cross safely.

And that's just what he did.

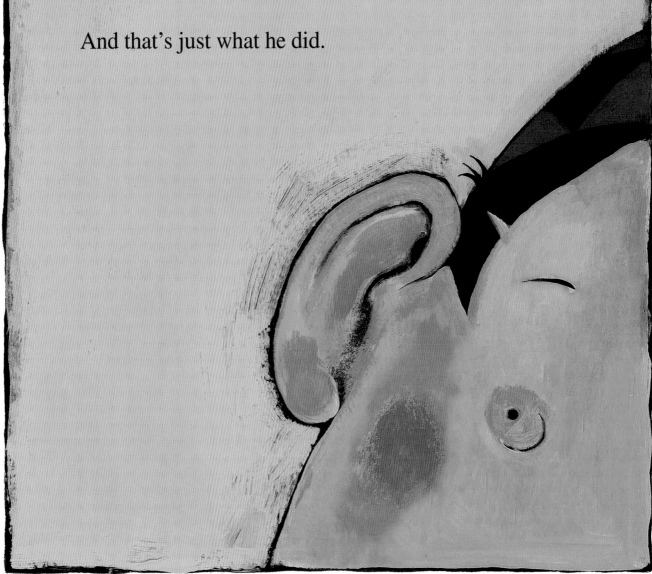

Then he skipped down the road towards the other village.

Just outside that village he came upon a crowd of people who were standing in a field, and he went up to them to see what they were doing. As he drew near, he heard them saying "Oooo" and "Ahhh" and "Ohhh," and he saw that they looked quite frightened.

He went up to one of the men and said, "Why are you saying 'Oooo' and 'Ahhh' and 'Ohhh,' and why are you all so frightened?"

"Oh dear me!" said the man. "There is a terrible, dangerous animal in this field, and we are all very frightened because it might attack us!"

"Where is the terrible, dangerous animal?" asked the boy, looking around.

"Oh! Be careful! Be careful!" cried the people.

But the clever boy asked again, "Where is the terrible, dangerous animal?"

And so the people pointed to the middle of the field.

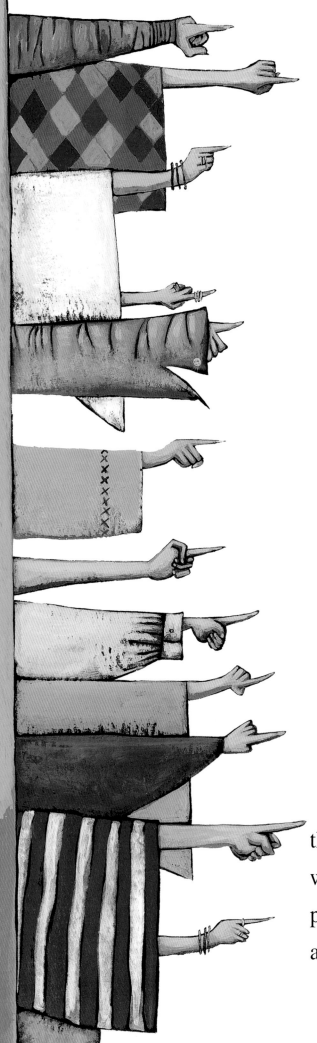

And when the boy looked where they pointed, he saw a very large ...

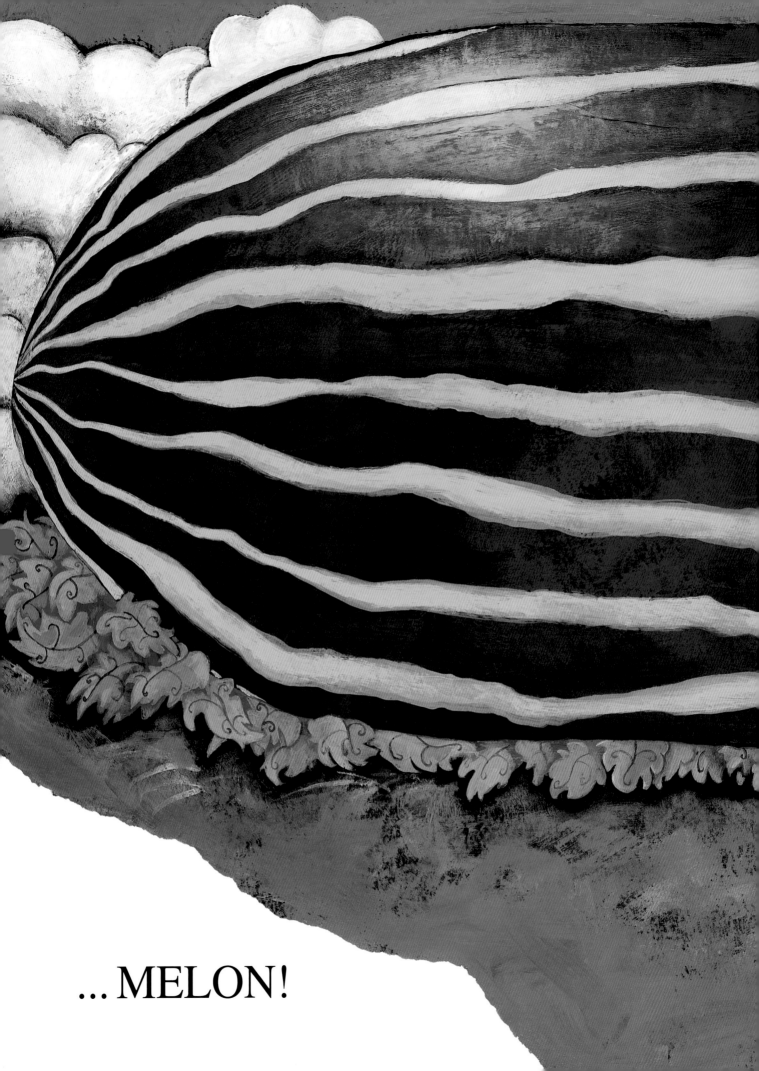

...MELON!

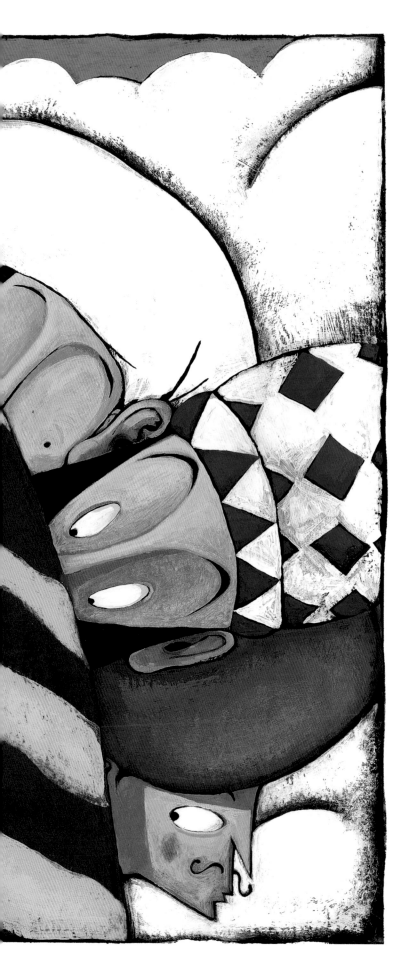

"That's not a terrible, dangerous animal!" laughed the boy.

"Yes, it is! It is!" cried the people. "Keep away! It might bite you!"

Now the boy saw that these people were very silly indeed, so he said to them, "I'll go and kill this dangerous animal for you."

"No, no!" cried the people. "It's too terrible! It's too dangerous! It might bite you! Oooo! Ahhh! Ohhh!"

But the boy went right up to the melon, took a knife out of his pocket, and cut a large slice out of it.

The people were astonished.

"What a brave boy!" they said. "He's killed the terrible, dangerous animal!"

As they spoke, the boy took a bite out of the large
slice of melon. It tasted delicious!

"Look!" cried the people. "Now he's eating the terrible, dangerous animal! He must be a terrible, dangerous boy!"

As the boy walked away from the middle of the field, waving his knife and eating the melon, the people ran away, saying, "Don't attack us, you terrible, dangerous boy. Keep away!"

At this the boy laughed again. He laughed and laughed and laughed. And then the people wondered why he was laughing, so they crept back.

"What are you laughing at?" they asked timidly.

"You're such a silly lot of people," said the boy. "You don't know that what you call a dangerous animal is just a melon."

"Melons are very nice to eat. We've got lots of them in our village ...

and everyone eats them."

Then the people became interested, and someone said,
"Well, how do we get melons?"

"You take the seeds out of a melon and you plant them
like this," he said, putting a few of the seeds in the ground.

"Then you give them water and look after them. And after a while, lots and lots of melons will grow from the seeds."

So the
people did
what the boy
showed
them.

And now, in all the fields of that village,
they have lots, and lots, and lots of melons.

They sell some,

and they eat some ...

and they give some away.

And that's why their village is
called Melon Village.

MELON VILLAGE

And just think. It all happened because a clever boy
was not afraid when a lot of silly people thought something
was dangerous just because they had never seen it before.

Other Books by Idries Shah

For Young Readers
The Boy Without a Name
The Silly Chicken
Neem the Half-Boy
The Farmer's Wife
The Lion Who Saw Himself in the Water
The Magic Horse
World Tales

Literature
The Hundred Tales of Wisdom
A Perfumed Scorpion
Caravan of Dreams
Wisdom of the Idiots
The Magic Monastery
The Dermis Probe

Novel
Kara Kush

Informal Beliefs
Oriental Magic
The Secret Lore of Magic

Humor
The Exploits of the Incomparable Mulla Nasrudin
The Pleasantries of the Incredible Mulla Nasrudin
The Subtleties of the Inimitable Mulla Nasrudin
Special Illumination

Travel
Destination Mecca

Human Thought
Learning How to Learn
The Elephant in the Dark
Thinkers of the East
Reflections
A Veiled Gazelle
Seeker After Truth

Sufi Studies
The Sufis
The Way of the Sufi
Tales of the Dervishes
The Book of the Book
Neglected Aspects of Sufi Study
The Commanding Self
Knowing How to Know

Studies of the English
Darkest England
The Natives are Restless

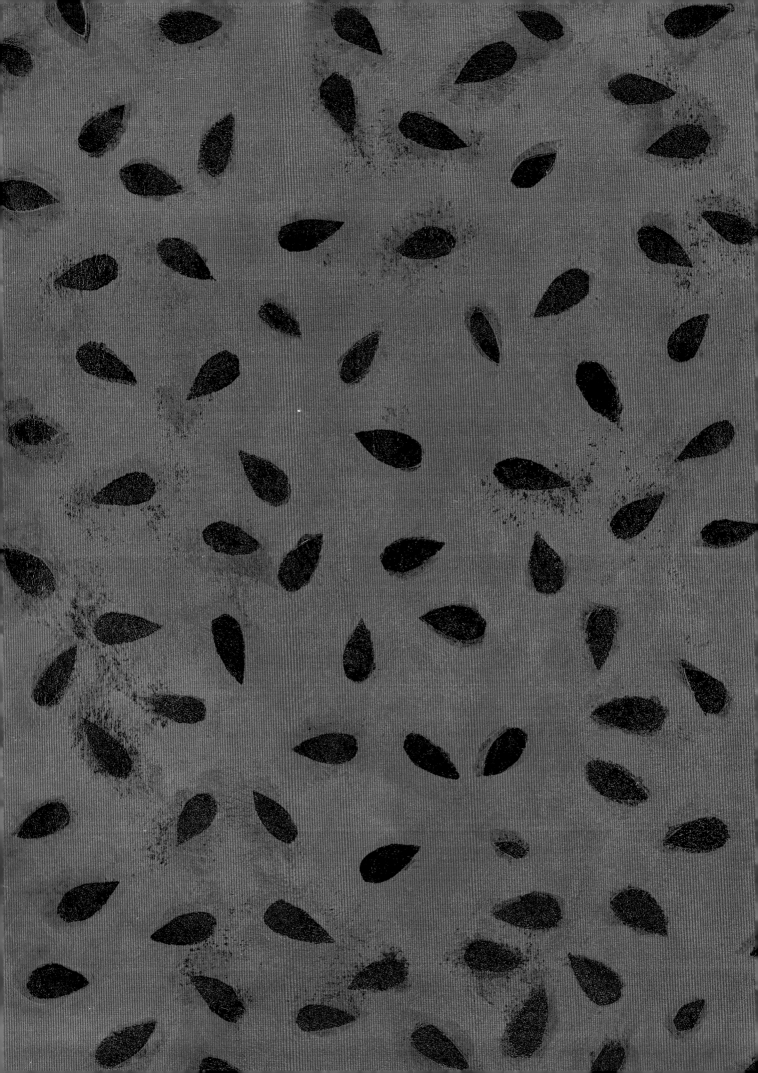